Fast40

Vol. 1
Needs, Wants and Desires

Cover and Layout Design by Dave Davis
Author Photo on page 82 by Brian Brown
Author Photo on back cover by Kristen Davis

Printed in the U.S.A.

First Printing, 2015

ISBN 978-1-944461-00-3
Library of Congress Control Number: 2015918588

PHO011020 PHOTOGRAPHY / Individual Photographers / Essays
FIC029000 FICTION / Short Stories (single author)

Panorama Creative Group
New Albany, IN 47150

www.PanoramaCG.com

To Kristen,

Without you, this book, along with the best part of my life, wouldn't be here.

Also by Dave Falkirk

Fast 40 – Vol. 2: Within, Without

Fast 40 – Vol. 3: The Shapes of Belief

For updates, free stories and other things of interest,
join up by clicking "newsletter" at www.davidfalkirk.com.
It comes complete with a 100-percent "no spam" guarantee.

Fast 40

Vol. 1
Needs, Wants and Desires

David Falkirk

PANORAMA
CREATIVE
GROUP

Table of Contents

It's left to those finding the photo,
without access to the true story, to
assign it meaning.

Preface

"A picture is worth a thousand words," it's said.

So, why only 250 per photo in this book? Where's the other 750? Who do you think you are, Falkirk? What kind of rip-off is this?

Don't worry. I'll get to that.

For me, the idea of a photograph has always been fascinating. While they can certainly be altered (Photoshop and Instagram have practically made a game of it), the goal of a photograph is to freeze a moment in time. Beyond memory and beyond the circumstances, the photo freezes a moment in time, perfect and forever. After the moment is gone, after the subject is gone, after the photographer is gone, the photo remains. If not properly documented, it can become divorced from the time and subject it captured, as those who remember the circumstances move along and shuffle off. It's left to those finding the photo, without access to the true story, to assign it meaning.

So, the idea behind this book, and its sister volumes, was to cut out the middleman of time, and give meaning to photos I've taken, regardless of what actually happened.

Sure, I could have picked each photo clean, leaving nothing but bones, but that's rude. I've found that 250 is a great length for a project like this. It gets the ball rolling. I've tried to give a complete view into each moment, but there's still room for movement.

What happens next? That's up to you.

There are another 750 words left.◐

Needs, Wants and Desires

Even just typing,
he was three times
the man I'll ever be.

Typewriter

My grandfather's typewriter sits in the corner, mocking me.

I should really put it away. All it does is remind me that I'm not the man he was; I never have been and probably never will be.

He fought in a war. He raised a family. He covered stories for newspapers, sometimes under death threats, and wrote several books on this typewriter he left me in his will, which now sits on my bookshelf.

I have access to computers and machines he would have killed for. No one is shooting at me, literally or figuratively. No one is depending on me to write the book I know is in me, but can't seem to pry out of my cobwebbed mind.

I tried, just for fun, to type a page on his typewriter. It left my fore arms burning and my fingertips numb, and a page full of typos. Even just typing, he was three times the man I'll ever be.

What are my excuses when compared to someone like him? They're lame. I'm lame.

I remember telling him I wanted to be a writer, like him. I remember him smiling at me, telling me that he'd love to have another writer in the family.

He died before I wrote anything I'd want him to read.

Now, his ghost fills the room. His typewriter sits, collecting dust. But his ghost is friendly. He wouldn't want me to simply copy him. He'd want me to write *my* story.

So, I begin again. Again. ✺

...there was nothing to do
but fill sandbags in an effort
to divert the worst of it away
from the most vulnerable.

Rain

It was welcome at first, the rain. It had been a dry season, and the rain soaked into the parched soil as fast as the ground could manage.

The rain lasted for hours, and everyone was happy.

The rain lasted for days, and everyone grew less happy.

Mrs. Gillian, living in her house by the creek bed, was the first to feel it. She watched, helpless, as the creek expanded from a trickle to a stream to a flow to a flood. She watched in horror as it left the banks and crept towards her house. She watched from the back seat of her son's car as he drove her from the house she and her husband had built so many years ago. She hoped she'd see it again. She hoped there would be something left.

Soon, the whole town was feeling what Mrs. Gillian had felt, as there seemed to be no end to the rain. The weather forecasters began their reports with apologies, as if they were to blame for the rains and the flood.

It would have been easier if they *were* to blame, because there would be a way to stop it. As it was, though, there was nothing to do but fill sandbags in an effort to divert the worst of it away from the most vulnerable.

And in the end, even the most stalwart among us realized that there was nothing to do but wait. Wait, and see what was left at the end.◐

She was special, in that way great
people are. And I was not.

Attraction

I hated her as much as I wanted to *be* her.

The impossibility of hating her made me hate her all the more.

My sister was two years older than me, but always seemed light years ahead of me. Not just because she got to do everything first — she "blossomed," as mom phrased it, more than two years before I did, and it looked better on her than it ever would on me — but because she just was *better* at life.

She had the best boyfriends, and even when she broke up with them, they were still her friends, somehow. As a teenager, that's impossible, but she pulled it off. Teachers loved her, not because she kissed their ass — she didn't — but because they recognized how great she was, just as everyone else did.

She had a grace that eluded me, not simply in the way she moved — although there was that — but how she related to people, and how people were drawn to her. Everything seemed to come easily for her, while I lumbered through life, leaving a debris field in my wake.

She was special, in that way *great* people are. And I was not.

I loved her. Everyone loved her. But there was always this bitter little core of my heart that hated her for everything she was that I wasn't.

So, when I opened the door and saw her, soaking wet, shivering on my doorstep, looking like her world had imploded, I had decidedly mixed feelings. ✸

"You're a poet," Cody said,
putting up another flyer.
Bam bam bam bam.

Posted

I'm sweatin' my balls off, Tommy," Cody said, using the hammer tacker to affix another flyer onto another utility pole. He used the same four-hit method — bam bam bam bam — on this one as he'd used on the last hundred.

"It'll be worth it," Tommy said. "I know it's a small show, but the right person hears us at the right time, and the world changes."

Cody admired Tommy's positive attitude. If it hadn't been for Tommy spearheading their practices and gigs, their band, the Train Spotters, would never have made it out of the garage. Times like these, though, being Tommy's friend was exhausting.

"All I know is Dennis and Jason better be plastering this much on their blocks," Cody said. "It's, like, 140 degrees today."

"We're paying our dues," Tommy said. "We have to give our biographers some stories, man."

"Oh, we've got biographers now?"

"We will," he said. "And what's a better story? 'We mixed something on the computer in our bedrooms, put it on YouTube and got discovered,' or 'We pounded the streets in the summer sun, trying to get people to hear us play'?"

"You're a poet," Cody said, putting up another flyer. Bam bam bam bam.

"C'mon, you know that Jagger and Richards and Lennon and McCartney and Townsend and Daltry and all the rest did exactly what we're doing now."

"Has anyone from the last 50 years do it?"

"Yeah," Tommy said. "*WE DID.*"

And, for a moment, Cody believed him. ✺

A little short-term pain, sure,
but from a long-term perspective,
it was the right thing to do.

Street

He had nothing to feel guilty about, he thought. Things happen. Times change.

People change.

He walked down the street, trying to clear his head, but the argument replayed over and over in his mind. No matter how fast he walked, he couldn't outrun it; he just carried it with him.

He wanted out. He was tired of fighting. He was tired of throwing good energy after bad. He wanted to try something new, something that felt like it could *grow* instead of just fighting to survive. He wanted to be excited again. Was that so bad? Everyone only gets so many trips around the sun.

It would be better for everyone, he thought. He was being *brave*, actually, no matter what names he had been called earlier. He was being the one with the guts to call it, to say what was actually going on, rather than pretend everything was fine. He did it so that they *both* could be free to do something that would make them happier in the long run. A little short-term pain, sure, but from a long-term perspective, it was the right thing to do.

As he walked, it started to sprinkle. He realized he was a mile away from his car, which was parked back by the shop. It hadn't looked like rain when he started his walk, but the clouds were dark and threatened a downpour.

This is not *an omen*, he thought, turning around to go back for shelter. ⟳

Jon saw him yawn, saw him
stink-eye witnesses, saw him
joke with his attorney, who
returned the laugh.

Courthouse

C'mon, Jon," his father said. "The sooner we get there, the sooner this'll be over."

Jon knew his dad meant well, but he also knew that it wasn't true. Their schedule — their *lives* for the past 10 months — had been totally dependent on the schedule of the courtroom. Dependent on the judge, on the lawyers and on Edward Spilling.

Always Spilling.

For the rest of his life, Jon would always remember his 16th year as the one Spilling stole from him. He stole his mother and his notion that good always beat evil. On the day Edward Spilling burst into their home, looking for a place to hide after a robbery gone wrong, Jon had stopped seeing the world one way and started seeing it another.

He was glad that Spilling was being sentenced today. He had seen him every day for a month as the trial went on. Jon saw him yawn, saw him stink-eye witnesses, saw him joke with his attorney, who returned the laugh.

Jon wanted to kill them both right then and there.

He knew, that he'd see Spilling again after this, when Spilling was up for parole — the prosecutor warned them that there probably would be parole hearings — Jon and his dad would have to testify if they didn't want Spilling to breathe free air.

After three hours of waiting in the courtroom, the judge finally came to read the sentence. Twenty years for taking Jon's mother.

He felt his father wince beside him. ⟳

There was the one, last option.
The one he had fought.
The one he had promised
himself was off limits.

Fuel

This shouldn't be a thing, Shane thought as he pulled up to the gas pump.

But it was. Shane knew exactly how much he had in his bank account, and he knew filling up the tank was going to take a sizable chunk of his current net worth. And he knew, at his age, that was just sad.

As he picked up the pump handle and swiped his debit card, he knew he had to make some money. The truck was on its last legs, and if it broke down, he didn't have a lot of options.

As the tank filled and the numbers rose higher, Shane counted each meal he'd have to scrimp on or skip all together. He hadn't felt this way since he was a teenager and had counted every cigarette and every fill-up. Back then, though, he had parents and a safety net. He didn't have to count each meal.

That life felt like someone else's now.

He decided he'd fill it up half-way. That would do for a couple of days, he thought, and maybe he'd come up with an idea.

He knew, though, that he wouldn't.

There was the one, last option. The one he had fought. The one he had promised himself was off limits.

He sighed, replaced the pump handle and walked over to the pay phone — the station had the last pay phone in town.

He dialed the number from memory.

"Joe, it's Shane," he said. "I'll do it." ↺

Andrew thought, in retrospect,
that such a concentrated
experience might have been
a mistake.

Cake

G od! It's like you don't even want to *get* married!"

"Not when you're like this, I don't!"

And there it was, hanging in the air between them, non-returnable.

Angela and Andrew had been out all day, making their wedding plans. They both had difficult schedules, so they had taken the day and made every appointment they could in one day. Andrew thought, in retrospect, that such a concentrated experience might have been a mistake.

They had been to the chapel, they had been to the reception venue, they had been to the restaurant where they planned to have the rehearsal dinner, and they had been to the jeweler to get the rings sized. He had heard "Angela and Andrew - how cute!" at each and every venue. And now, they were outside the bakery that specialized in wedding cakes; they had made the cake at Angela's best friend's wedding.

They tasted cakes. They looked at designs. They discussed prices. Andrew wasn't trying to be mean, or unenthusiastic, or unsupportive. He just sincerely, in his heart of hearts, couldn't have cared less, except to think that the money she wanted to spend on a cake would go a long way towards a down payment on a house.

When Angela called him on his apparent lack of interest as they left, he spoke his mind — that he felt more like a prop than an participant.

And now, they looked at each other, deciding what to do next.

"I'm tired," he finally said. ✺

Kevin felt guilty about what
happened, even though,
rationally, he knew he had
done nothing wrong.

Pizza

It's only awkward if I let it be awkward, Kevin thought as the pizza arrived.

"Here we go, guys," Nate said. "You helped us move, so now stuff yourselves with pizza. It's the American way!"

"Cheaper than movers," Allan said, helping himself to the first piece.

Kevin had been happy to help Nate and Emily move; Nate had been one of the first to volunteer when Kevin moved the previous year, so it was a favor he had been glad to repay. He had been ready to pitch in wherever needed, and had found himself in the bedroom picking up boxes.

And then he picked up *that* box.

Kevin felt guilty about what happened, even though, rationally, he knew he had done nothing wrong. Nate and Emily should have put that box aside to take themselves. And they *damn* well should have made sure the bottom wouldn't fall out when it was picked up, for fear of exposing an honestly impressive array of items better left unseen.

The only thing that could have made the situation worse would have been for Emily to come into the room at that exact moment — which, of course, was exactly what had happened. Kevin didn't know how long he stood there, holding a suddenly empty, bottomless box, Emily staring at him, and then at the "special" debris surrounding him on the floor.

All he knew was that neither had been able to look the other in the eye for the rest of the move. ◐

...but I knew the risks
— the ramifications —
of failure demanded that failure
would not occur.

Empty

The room was empty, but that was impossible. The room *couldn't* be empty.

I searched to see if the unit was hiding somehow, but I knew that there was simply no place for it to hide. It was gone.

Impossible, but that was the reality.

There were eight redundant levels of security to keep this from happening. Eight! They only wanted to build in three levels at the beginning of the project, but I'd insisted. They laughed at my "paranoia," but I knew the risks — the ramifications — of failure demanded that failure would not occur.

And, yet, it had.

After I sounded the alarm, I examined the room while I waited for the emergency response team. There were no signs of violence. Nothing was broken. The unit, somehow, had simply opened the door and walked out.

I would have felt better if it *had* broken out. At least then we'd know what we were dealing with.

It was the A.I. — I was sure of it. I hadn't wanted to use Johnson's shoddy programming, but I had no choice. To take the unit to the next level, it had to have some measure of adaptability. Johnson said he had lobotomized the A.I., though, so we wouldn't get a repeat of last year. Being able to circumvent this much security, however, showed we were dealing with something smarter.

Then, as the ERT showed up, I heard something behind me and I realized my mistake.

We couldn't get the door closed in time.◑

They had nothing to worry about
from him. He'd given up
on them years earlier.

Understand

They didn't understand, and he couldn't *make* them understand. He had made multiple attempts, and had failed each and every time.

He stopped trying long ago.

The only reason he spoke to himself was to get the ideas out of his head, out into the open, into the light of day where they didn't seem so massive. Adding sunlight to drive the shadow away. No one else could understand him, but maybe if he spoke the words, gave them weight, he could wrestle with them.

The worst part was that *he* didn't understand them, either. The words were just there, in his head, unbidden.

Speaking them aloud didn't help, though. It just drove people away. He saw how they looked at him. He watched them cross the street when they saw him coming, or, if they couldn't cross the street, find something fascinating to look at on their phone, or anywhere he wasn't.

They had nothing to worry about from him. He'd given up on them years earlier.

There were times he thought himself crazy; he *wished* he was. He tried to convince himself that the problem was in his head. An accident of biochemistry.

He tried writing the words out, first on paper, but then on larger and larger canvases, until he was working with spray paint on walls.

He stood back and looked, but the words still made no sense.

He didn't speak the language. There were times when he wondered if he spoke any language at all. ✪

The eggs start burning, forgotten,
when you ask if there's anything
she's not telling you.

Five Minutes

Five minutes doesn't sound like a lot of time. A lot can happen in five minutes, though. You can listen to a song, read a story about last night's game or make a surprisingly complete breakfast.

You can be timing yourself making that breakfast, to prove a point to your daughter, when your wife tells you she can't do "this" anymore.

The toast pops out of the toaster when you ask her what she just said. She says that you heard her correctly. She's tired of her marriage to you, tired of marriage in general, and that two people sometimes just grow in different directions. It's harmful to pretend otherwise

The microwave beeps, telling you that the bacon's done. You don't hear it, though, because now you're asking your wife — who'll apparently be your *ex*-wife in the near future — if she's considered what this revelation might do to the daughter you both share. She tells you that it'll be better for her in the long run if her parents are honest with her now. You ask how "honest" it is if this is the first you're hearing about it.

The eggs start burning, forgotten, when you ask if there's anything she's not telling you. If there's any*one* she's not telling you about. If there's a reason this is happening so suddenly.

The way she hesitates tells you everything you need to know.

You hear your daughter coming downstairs into a new world that came into being five minutes ago. ✪

Everything seemed so large,
just as the world would seem
to a child.

Church

It was the first time Erin had set foot in a church in the better part of a decade. She wouldn't have been there at all if her best friend's daughter wasn't being christened. The hallmark of a true friend, she knew, was someone willing to get over themselves for special occasions.

As she walked into the ornate, cavernous building, she felt overwhelmed. Old churches were designed to do that, she supposed; in the presence of God, one should be in a state of awe. She loved the stained glass, the tapestries, the statues — she had to admit that she loved the grandeur of it all. Everything seemed so large, just as the world would seem to a child.

Erin was there early, so she had time to get a closer look at some of the artwork. Were the artists paid to do a job, she wondered, or were they simply moved to raise their artistic "voices" to give glory to the Lord?

She felt oddly at peace in the church as she found a seat in the front row. She had been raised in a church like this one, and began to wonder why she had stayed away so long.

Lost in thought, Erin didn't notice the elderly lady until the lady poked her hard in the shoulder. "You're in my seat," she said, motioning her to get up, glaring at her until she moved. At that point, it was starting to come back to her why she'd left.🌀

"Don't say 'warmth,'" Leah said.
"A hipster would say 'warmth.'"

LP

"You are such a hipster," Leah said.

"I'm not a hipster," Pete said.

"Said the hipster with the mustache telling me that vinyl is an 'under-appreciated' medium. Dude, you are the very definition of 'hipster.' I could look it up in a dictionary, and there you'd be, under 'hipster,' explaining why dead-tree dictionaries are better than online dictionaries."

"All I said was that LPs offer an extra dynamic range that digital media can't match," Pete said as he went over to the shelf and pulled out an album seemingly at random. Leah had know him long enough, though, to know that the "random" album would be one specially selected to make his argument — in this case, it was 1983's *Peter Gabriel Plays Live*.

He took one of the albums — it was a two disk set — carefully, achingly slowly, out of its sleeve, placed it on the turntable, started it spinning, took out a felt brush out to knock off any dust, and then placed the needle — *achingly* slowly — on the first track. With a slight pop, "The Rhythm of the Heat" started playing.

"Hear that?" Pete asked. "That…."

"Don't say 'warmth,'" Leah said. "A hipster would say 'warmth.'"

"I was going to say 'ineffable quality.'"

"That's worse," Leah said. "I hear pops, crackles and something I couldn't listen to in the car or jogging."

"It's all about practicality with you, isn't it?"

"Obviously not," she said. "I'm here with *you*, aren't I?"

And then she kissed him. ✪

It was a simple thing,
that bit of metal...

Ring

A fter he washed his hands, he looked at his wedding ring, laying next to the sink. And, for whatever reason, he then *really* looked at it, taking in what it meant.

There was the physicality of it — a circular band that was the only jewelry that he regularly wore, that had worn a slight groove in his fourth finger, and left its inverse tan when it was off.

There was the societal function of it — proclaiming that he was spoken for, that he was pair bonded, theoretically, for life.

There was the spiritual aspect of it — a band that never begins and never ends, but continues both finite and infinite.

But what was the true meaning of it, he wondered. What did it mean to *him,* as a person, as a primate on a rock revolving around a continuing nuclear explosion hurtling through space for as long as was allowed?

It was a simple thing, that bit of metal, but when he stopped to think about it — *really* stopped and *really* contemplated — it simply reminded him of her. Even when she wasn't there, she was, in a way. She had a permanent spot in his mind and in his soul, of course, but the ring was a physical reminder, ever so slight, that she was there for him, always. A statement of purpose and a statement of fact.

Mindful of all this, he put the ring back on his finger, and felt it settle into the groove it had formed. ✪

What if someone who wasn't as
conscientious as he was found it?

Drive

Marty didn't usually go to the park during his lunch hour, but the day was so nice that it called to him to go enjoy it. As he walked around the lake, making the final turn back towards his car, he saw it — a USB thumb drive laying in the grass.

The small piece of tech almost seemed to jump out at him. It probably hadn't been there long; someone else would have picked up, he imagined.

It was in a place where people liked to lay and soak up sun on a day like this, and probably had fallen out of a pocket.

Marty picked it up. It was an older drive; it only held two gigabytes. Tiny by modern standards — Marty had one on his key ring that held 32 gigabytes and only paid $20 for it. Still, the curiosity was there. What was on the drive? It wouldn't hold a lot of media, but it could hold oceans of pages. Was it someone's novel? An important report? Backups of emails from a lover? Pictures of the owner's kids? MP3s of a favorite album?

He wondered if he should leave it where it was. Maybe the owner would come back looking for it once it had been missed. But, what if it rained? What if someone who wasn't as conscientious as he was found it?

Marty put it in his pocket and decided to see if he could find the owner from the contents. He enjoyed a puzzle. ✪

"To think that this is a piece of
something so... unreachable."

Lunar

It looks unreal. It felt unreal.

It *couldn't* be real.

Jenny looked at the stone in the exhibit in front of her, unbelieving.

The rock, part of the traveling exhibit, was from the Moon, brought back by Apollo 16, decades earlier. She had never seen it, didn't even know it was part of the exhibit. And yet, she knew every bump, every grain, every pit, every shadow on its surface.

She had dreamt about *that* stone for weeks.

The recurring dream was curious at first, but after 23 straight nights, she had started worrying for her sanity. The dream had no subtext or characters or other symbols. It was just the stone — *this* stone — floating in front of her, and her staring at it, unable to touch it.

Just as she was doing at that very moment, unable to touch it behind its protective glass.

After the third night, she consulted a dream dictionary and read that the symbol of "moon" could mean a hidden part of yourself wants to emerge, or it could signify changing moods. None of those really connected with her. And, besides, it wasn't the Moon she was dreaming of. It was this *piece* of it

"It's something, isn't it?" said the old woman next to her. Jenny hadn't noticed her approach. "To think that this is a piece of something so… unreachable."

The woman spoke of physical miles, but to Jenny, the rock had traveled a much greater distance — from her dream into her reality.◖

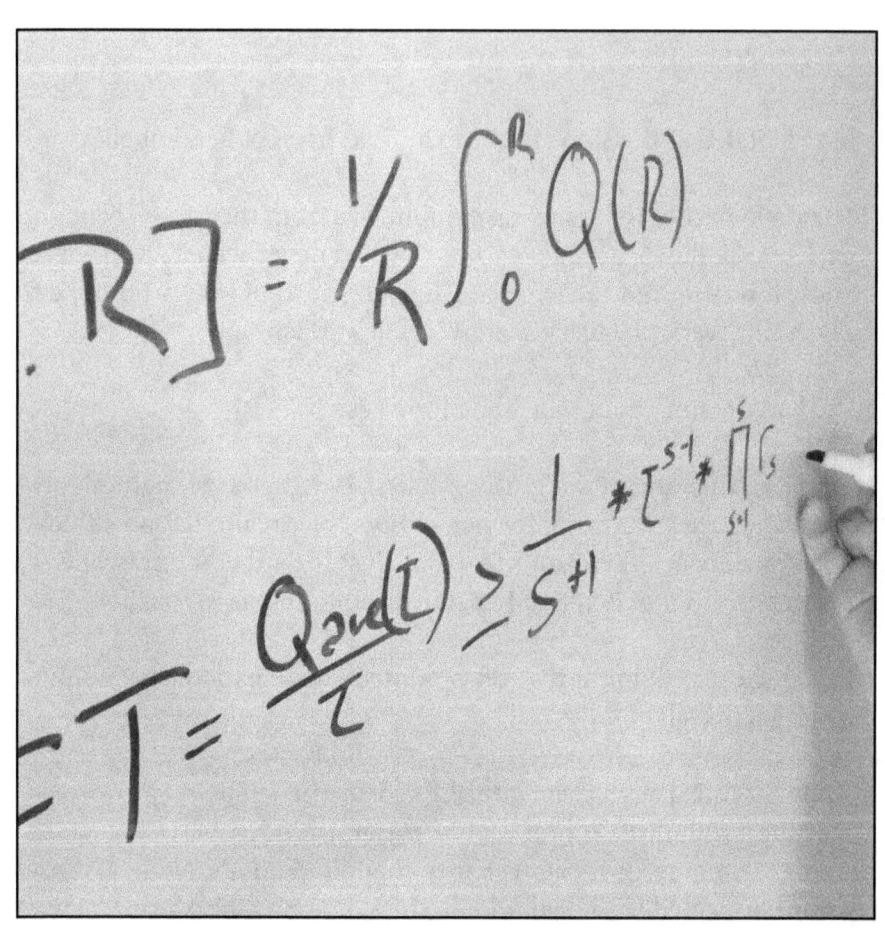

There was, after all,
pleasure in pack mentality.

Exposed

Grant knew that his equation was wrong even as he wrote it on the whiteboard. He could feel them waiting for him to finish so they could tear into it.

He had explained to Dr. Cornet his math wasn't done yet ("Not done to my satisfaction" was the way Grant phrased it, trying to salvage what little dignity he could out of this disaster), but Cornet told him to put up what he had, and let the rest of the staff take a look. "Maybe someone will be able to provide the missing piece that will make it come together," he said. Grant liked Dr. Cornet, but he also knew the man didn't comprehend the reality of the situation; almost every member of the group lived to make the rest suffer. There was no invoking the Golden Rule here; that would require a prohibitive level of hypocrisy.

Grant was no exception. When Leon showed up unprepared to defend his findings two weeks earlier, Grant had been more than happy to pile on. There was, after all, pleasure in pack mentality. Now, out of the corner of his eye, he could see Leon smiling, making notes.

But Leslie Bracken wouldn't leave much for Leon or the rest to pick over.

She was the only one who didn't take joy in destroying her teammates, though; she did it because she believed it was the right thing to do. She was smart. Frighteningly smart.

It was one of things Grant loved about her. ✺

It was unnatural,
shooting through tunnels
under the world above.

Subway

He hated the subway. It was unnatural, shooting through tunnels under the world above.

His job was what it was, and where it was, though, and the subway was the best of a bad set of choices.

He looked at the people surrounding him — it was unnatural being around *this* many people, pressed together this closely, underground. The claustrophobia was bad enough — being in tunnels deep beneath the surface — but all the people competing for precious space just added to the rising panic he felt each and every day, both ways, during his commute.

And no one else seemed to share his distress. No one had the wild-eyed look he fought to keep off his own features, but always sensed he failed at hiding. Were they just better at it than he imagined he was? Or did they really, truly not care?

He didn't care for the city in general. It was too big. Too complicated. Too many things moving in too many directions. Too easy to feel lost, too easy to not see a familiar face for days on end. He had never made the connections he had hoped to make.

He envied the people he saw traveling together in the tunnels. Envied them so badly it ached. "Envy is counting someone else's blessings," his mother had said. He was tired of feeling like the window dressing in someone else's story.

Enough.

He decided to do something about it, as soon as he re-emerged into the sunlight. ◐

...his wife always called him a "frustrated farmer," while she called Josh an "indoor cat."

Content

"We need content for our Website, Dad," Josh said. "We need to become sticky."

"We're a stump removal business," Adam said. "What kind of 'content' could we possibly have, and what the hell does 'sticky' mean? We just need our phone number out there and maybe some photos. We don't need to be Yahoo or something."

Adam saw his son roll his eyes at that.

"We want to separate ourselves from the competition," Josh said, heading off the "respect your elders" lecture headed his way. "It's not just, 'We can remove your stump.' It's, 'Why *we* should be the ones to remove your stump.'"

Adam wanted to work with his son — he had dreamed of an "Ellis & Son" sign the moment Josh was born. But it had been apparent early on that it would take some work to make that happen. Adam liked to get outside and get his hands dirty; his wife always called him a "frustrated farmer," while she called Josh an "indoor cat." The boy didn't like to get dirty. He'd rather read than fish, and when he discovered computers, it was difficult to pry him away from the keyboard.

So, Adam took advantage of the rare overlapping interests whenever he could. They bonded over college basketball. They both enjoyed Clint Eastwood films. And, when Josh suggested developing a Website for the business, Adam gladly took him up on it.

What he didn't expect, though, was how thorough his son was.

He was both proud and confused. ↻

Bill was in a mood, and Evan didn't
know if he was going to be able to
talk him out of it this time.

Virtues

C'mon, man — 'patience is a virtue' and all that," Evan said.

"You know what else is a virtue? Having the balls to do something that needs doing."

Bill was in a mood, and Evan didn't know if he was going to be able to talk him out of it this time.

"I'm not sure that's actually a virtue," Evan said. "Especially when it comes to your ex-wife's boyfriend."

Bill whirled on Evan. "First, she's not my ex-wife. Not yet. We're just separated. Second, the fact that she found a boyfriend so soon means that she already *had* a boyfriend. They're just now brave enough to go public with it. What's there to be 'patient' about?"

Evan wondered if Bill didn't have a point. Just because he had a temper didn't mean he was wrong. But, even if he was right, what would be the point of letting him get into trouble that, as mad as he was, would be bad for everyone concerned?

"Cool down for a minute," he finally said. "You're going to do something you'll regret. Let's go get a beer." Evan regretted saying that last bit; alcohol probably wasn't the missing ingredient needed to avoid this particular disaster.

"Don't 'handle' me, Evan," Bill said. "Haven't you ever felt the need to deliver a richly deserved ass kicking?"

"Fine," he said, tired of playing counselor. "Your temper is the reason she ended it with you in the first place. Now, go prove her right, you idiot." ◑

...they both knew he couldn't have
formed a deeply held belief
on the matter.

Chips

"What do you think? 'Bonfire' or 'Red Gumball'?"

Will looked at the paint color chip and knew that, whatever he said, Lisa would probably choose the opposite. He based this on 10 years of experience with the woman. If he really had a strong opinion about something, she'd listen. Since he had never heard the phrase "accent wall" until she brought it up three days ago, though, they both knew he couldn't have formed a deeply held belief on the matter.

"I dunno," he said. "Isn't the 'Bonfire' kinda… pinkish?"

"Yeah, but you wouldn't want something that's *too* red."

Sometimes, during a situation like this, Will wondered if he had lost some freedom in his life. Would his father have ever debated "Bonfire" or "Red Gumball" with his mother? His grandfather certainly wouldn't have. So, Will wondered, was he the domesticated male? Or, worse, the *overly* domesticated male?

He thought back to his bachelor days, where no one could tell him what to do; if he wanted a bright red wall, by God, there would be a red wall there as soon as he got around to it.

Then he looked at Lisa, and remembered something else about his bachelorhood — he had been looking for someone like her the entire time. A beautiful partner. "Freedom," he knew, was vastly overrated.

He'd gotten lucky, and if that meant living with a pinkish wall, so be it.

"'Bonfire' is fine," he said.

"Actually, 'Red Gumball' is kind of growing on me now…." ✺

"Looks dangerous," Molly said,
and hated herself a little for it.

Vulcan

O h, would you look at this…."

As they walked down the sidewalk, Molly had seen the motorcycle before James did, so she had a moment to mentally prepare herself. It had been a nice dinner and a nice night for a stroll.

And now their night was about to have a nice motorcycle join them.

"Oooh, man," he said, letting go of her hand as they approached it. "It's a Vulcan 800, and it's soooo cherry."

She hated when James referred to things as "cherry."

He was a good man, a good husband, a good father, but was a little boy when it came to motorcycles. He had one when they started dating, and he had reluctantly parted with it when they had their first child. There was still a motorcycle-shaped hole in his heart that she had come to realize would never fully close.

He circled the bike, taking it in, ticking off its attributes.

"Looks like a 1997," he said. "Has a 805 cc liquid-cooled V-twin, five speed transmission with… yep, the slap shift."

At times, Molly felt like the buzzkill of the relationship. James had an enthusiasm for things that she couldn't quite muster; this would be one of those things.

"Whoever has this is a lucky man," James said, more to himself than her.

"Looks dangerous," Molly said, and hated herself a little for it.

"Yeah," he said, taking her hand again. He stole one glance over his shoulder as they walked away. ✿

"That's not even good poetry,"
Kate said.

Hollow

"Of all the ways to spend a Saturday, this has got to be one of the dumbest," Kate said.

"Would you at least *try* to get into the spirit?" Ellen asked. "It actually could be fun…"

"Scavenger hunts are dumb," Kate said. "We're not teenagers."

They were on a nature trail near the home of their friends Margaret and Henry, who had come up with the idea. The trail, to the best of Ellen's reckoning, was where the next clue would be. "We're not ready for the nursing home, either. What's your deal?"

"My 'deal' is I'm traipsing around a trail in heels looking for clues to a dumb 'prize' I don't care about," Kate said. "Why are we friends with them, anyway?"

Why am I friends with you? Ellen wondered. High school had been a long time ago, and while Kate had been her best friend since then, she was beginning to feel like they weren't a good fit for each other any more.

Ellen pulled the strip of paper and read the clue aloud again. "And there the next clue you'll see when you dare examine the mouth of the screaming tree," she said.

"That's not even good poetry," Kate said.

"Hey, check out that tree," Ellen said, pointing to one with a hollow that looked like an gaping mouth, complete with "teeth." "It looks like it's screaming! I'll be that's it," she said.

"Yay," Kate said.

It was at that moment when Ellen felt their friendship die. ↻

"Things might not have been
as 'efficient' as they are now,
but I knew how to work them."

Time

Joy looked at the parking lot's meter and wanted to cry.

"What's wrong, Mom?"

"Crystal, it's *frustrating*," Joy said. "It's like I've blinked and I'm living in a new country, where I don't speak the language anymore." She pointed at the lot meter. "I'm looking at it, and I have no idea what to do with this thing."

"It's not that hard, Mom," Crystal said. "You just take your debit card, and…."

"It wasn't that long ago that they had people in booths who took real, honest-to-God money," Joy said. "Sometimes, they'd even smile at you and tell you to have a good day. Now, what do we have? Credit cards and machines, and buttons and…"

"This is more efficient," Crystal said. "Now, it doesn't matter when you come back - you don't have to beat the meter."

"It's not just this," Joy said. "I have to remember how to turn on the TV and the cable box in the right order. Half the stuff on my radio is beyond me, and I have no idea what a 'bluetooth' is. Things might not have been as 'efficient' as they are now, but I knew how to work them."

She sighed and sat down on the bench beside the meter. "Don't listen to me," she said, seeing the worry in her daughter's eyes. "I'm just feeling old. Things move too fast for me to catch up."

"You've got me, Mom," Crystal said, taking out her debit card. "I can translate." ◐

Jeremy, who had failed upwards,
was territorial about the few
things he had in his domain.

Frame

Greg sat, fidgeting, in the chair across the desk from his boss. The chair, he decided, was intentionally defective. A spring poked him in the butt so there was no comfortable way to position himself.

His boss, Jeremy, was laying into him about some report Greg hadn't filed correctly. Greg knew that the report was practically meaningless, but was one of the few things over which Jeremy had control. Jeremy, who had failed upwards, was territorial about the few things he had in his domain.

As Jeremy's raged, Greg started looking around the office, trying to focus on something, *anything*, other than Jeremy's hissy fit.

His eyes finally came to rest on the picture frame on Jeremy's desk. He had no idea what the picture was; he could only see the back of the frame. Wife? Kids? Would someone actually marry and/or reproduce with Jeremy? What the hell would that be like?

As Jeremy railed on, Greg made a mental note to take his job search from "passive" to "active." He then went back to the photo. A yellowed photo of Jeremy and his dad with a fish? Was his dad responsible for Jeremy's personality? Was it a picture of a dog? Maybe it was the dog's birthday, with it wearing a cute birthday hat.

As Jeremy dismissed Greg or, more accurately, told him to "get out of my sight," Greg knew the main goal of his remaining time at the company to get a look at that photo. ◐

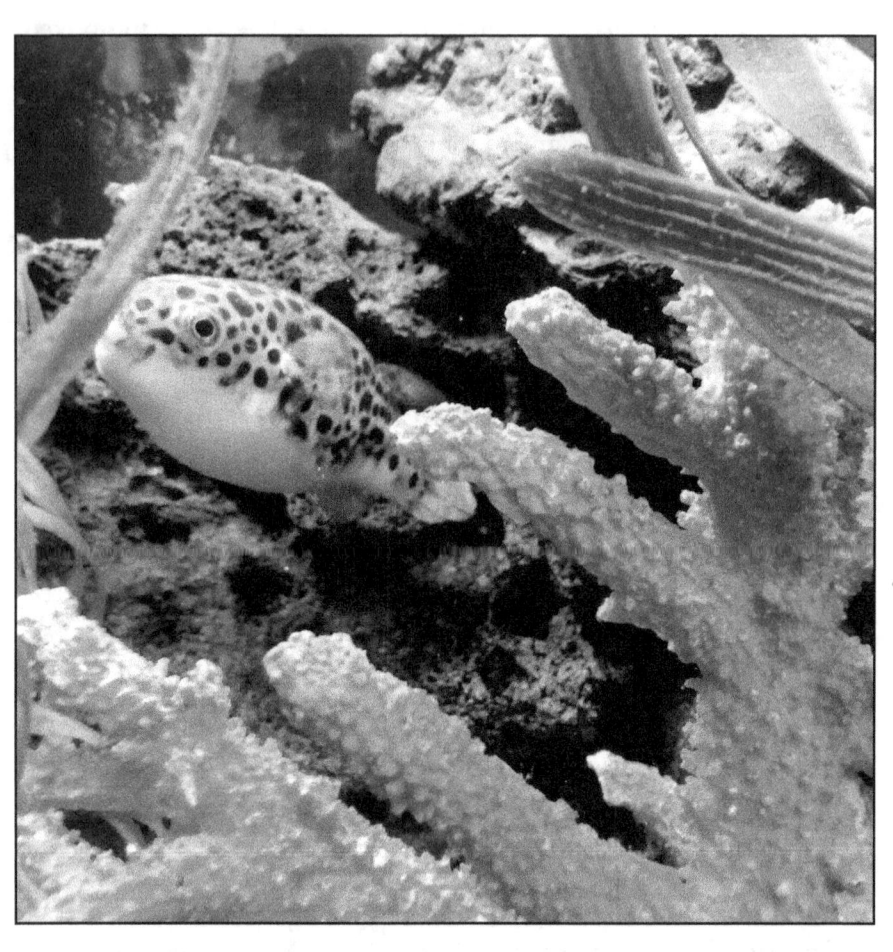

Barry found himself in
the waiting room on
a Tuesday afternoon, preparing
for a medical judgment.

Fish

Oh, for the life of a fish, Barry thought, looking at the aquarium. Not a fish in the ocean, where everything was designed to eat everything else. No, just a fish in a tank, in a doctor's office, thanks.

Barry didn't really know fish. He didn't know what the fat yellow-and-black spotted one he stared at was called. It seemed content. There's happiness in ignorance, he knew. He himself had been happy not being aware of his liver — since it had always worked, it had always been invisible. That was, until his doctor saw "shadow" on the x-ray.

More x-rays and CT scans followed in this frightening new hobby — "just so we know what we're looking at," the doctor said — and Barry found himself in the waiting room on a Tuesday afternoon, preparing for a medical judgment.

The fish was totally oblivious to all this, of course.

He wondered what it was like for the fish. What was its view of the strange faces it saw every day through the glass? Did it even notice? Was it afraid these strange creatures would eat it? If so, it was playing it cool. Swim like no one's watching.

He was tempted to tap the tank, but decided not to. Why alarm the fish? Why make it think something was out to get it?

Barry felt a tap on his shoulder. "Mr. Jacobs?" the nurse said. "The doctor's ready for you."

He envied that fish so much it hurt. ☙

"You shouldn't write in your books," she said. "That's for coloring books. You should keep your books nice."

Highlights

What are you *doing*?" It was the same tone in his mother's voice, Bobby thought, she would have had if she had caught him starting a fire over some oily rags.

"I'm reading," he said, startled and honestly puzzled over what she *thought* he was doing.

"You're writing in your book!"

"I'm highlighting stuff," he said. It hadn't occurred to him that the yellow florescent highlighter marks had been the cause of her distress.

"You shouldn't write in your books," she said. "That's for coloring books. You should keep your books nice."

He knew his mom had come from different circumstances. She had grown up poor, and Bobby had grown up comfortably. It was something that she took pride in, but it caused an inevitable gap between them.

"It's not disrespectful," he said. "It's *my* book. You could say I'm just personalizing it." She gave him a look that he recognized immediately. She didn't agree, but was debating whether to make it an issue.

"Come over here," he said. He handed her the highlighter, putting it in her hand when she didn't immediately take it. Bobby pointed at a passage in the book. "Highlight that sentence," he said. "It's a good one."

"I'm not…"

"Go ahead. Do it."

She looked at him, doubtfully, and after a hesitation, slowly, carefully, highlighted the sentence, and not a bit more.

"Felt good, didn't it?"

She handed back the highlighter and walked off, shaking her head a little. But he had seen her smile. ✿

It seemed silly when his father suggested a positive mental attitude, but Ricky didn't have anything to lose.

PMA

oday is going to be different, Ricky thought as the school bus got closer. Today, he was going to go in with the attitude that nothing could go wrong. It seemed silly when his father suggested a positive mental attitude, but Ricky didn't have anything to lose. "You can't control what other people do," his dad said; "you can only control how you react to it."

How he *wanted* to react — to bar the doors and burn the middle school to the ground — wasn't going to fly, so positive mental attitude it was.

As the bus got closer, Ricky reminded himself of everything he had going for him. He was smart, all his limbs worked… and he was sure there were other things, which eluded him as the bus pulled up.

He took a deep breath as the doors opened, and got on. The bus lurched ahead before he scoped out a seat, and even though he expected it — the same thing happened every day — he still had to grab the a seat back to stop from falling.

PMA, he thought as he looked for a place to sit in the nearly full bus.

Seats by girls were off the table, as were seats with older kids (especially Brent, who must have failed at least two grades to be *that* much bigger and meaner).

That left Chris, Terry and Shawn, none of whom looked eager to share their space.

"Sit down!" the always-annoyed bus driver yelled.

PMA, Ricky thought. ✺

A nap might make The Man return
faster. Sometimes that worked.

Dog

The Man had been gone for days. Luke got up and patrolled the house again, making the same circuit that he always did: kitchen, bedroom, kitchen, living room, kitchen, back door, kitchen, and back to the front door. How many times had he walked that path since The Man had left? Luke had no way of knowing.

Luke sniffed at the door again. He could smell Outside, and wished that, if The Man had left for good, he would have at least let him go Outside. Inside always smelled the same, unless The Man brought a kill home to share. For someone so slow, Luke had to admit The Man was an excellent hunter. He rarely left their den without returning with something to eat. The Man took most of the food, but Luke knew his place in the pack. It was good. He had never gone too hungry.

Luke sighed, and laid on his side, stretching his legs before relaxing. A nap might make The Man return faster. Sometimes that worked.

Just then, though, he saw the smaller house come closer and pull up next to the big house. One of the walls opened, and The Man stepped out.

Luke's heart exploded with joy. He hoped his tail showed how happy he was. The pack was whole again! He greeted The Man by trying to get in his face and smell if he had eaten.

"Luke, calm down, boy," The Man said. "I've only been gone 20 minutes, dude." ✪

Jack wondered what kind of
report HR would have to file if he
started throwing things at her.

Toys

I don't understand the toys," Marjorie said, her condescension practically dripping onto Jack's desk as she picked up the die-cast *Millennium Falcon*. "You're a grown man. Why do you have toys on your desk?"

Since a pithy answer didn't spring to mind, Jack decided to go on offense.

"Why does it matter to you?" he asked, snatching it back.

"It just looks… unprofessional," she said. "Do you *play* with them? Do you make little 'pew-pew' sounds?"

Not for the first time, Jack wished that Marjorie had more work to do, so she didn't feel so free to roam the office. "I just like looking at them. You have a cactus on your desk. Does *that* help your productivity?"

"My cactus is a living thing," she said. "Your toys are just… toys."

"I'm a designer. I need inspiration," Jack said. "You're a coder. Go code. Maybe the cactus will pitch in or something."

"Some of the guys around me have toys on their desks, too. Is it a guy thing? Are you all just… developmentally stunted or something?"

Jack wondered what kind of report HR would have to file if he started throwing things at her. He sincerely doubted anyone in the office would mind, but still. Paperwork.

"Tell you what," he said. "Let's arrange a play date between your cactus and the *Falcon*."

"Whatever," she said. As she walked away, Jack wondered what would happen if he clocked her in the back of her head with the *Falcon*. ✪

The majority of stars were hidden,
but they were still there.

Night

Her mother did her level best to make her afraid of the night.
"Be in before dark."
"Don't stay out too late."
"You don't know what's lurking out there in the dark."

Through her childhood, she'd taken all of that in. She was careful when and where she should be. She wasn't stupid. Her mother wasn't wrong; night is the time when the creeps come out to play.

But it was also the time the stars came out to play. There was nothing she liked so much as to be out in the country after the sun set, away from the city and its eternal, nagging glow, and watch the stars slowly come out. Venus usually the first, but all the rest would follow soon after.

She remembered the first time she saw the country stars, and she could easily imagine herself a girl in ancient Rome, or out in a remote village, or anywhere 10 miles from civilization, and just lose herself to the night sky.

Even now, in her neighborhood, out for an evening stroll, the night was like a blanket, hiding unkempt lawns or badly maintained fences. The majority of the stars were hidden, but they were still there.

She heard a rustling in some nearby bushes, breaking the spell she was under. It sounded too big to be a cat or some other easy-to-buy explanation. She sighed, silently unlocked her mace, made plans to travel out to the countryside that weekend, and got ready. ✺

Comes a time when you know
things aren't going to get better.

Kindness

It was a kindness, what I did.

They hate me, these townspeople, but I stand by what I've done. Before, faced with my "crime," I'd have agreed with those wanting to hang me, but now my "crime" isn't what keeps me up at night; the reason for it does.

The blizzard had been unearthly.

The food ran out first. There are ways around that; your palate gets less picky as your stomach gets more demanding. Water wasn't a problem, as long as there was enough fuel for a fire. The blizzard gave us water to last a lifetime.

It was the sickness that forced my hand. The girls caught it first — the lungs of the youngest are always the most vulnerable — then my boy, and then my wife. Why I didn't get it, I don't know. Hand to God, and the end, I *tried* to. I didn't want to be alone, and I *certainly* didn't want to do what I eventually had to.

The sickness showed no kindness.

My wife and I laid there in the dark, one of us always up to make sure the fire didn't die, and listened to them breathe, each breath more painful. We'd never seen anything like this sickness. Simply breathing became agony.

Comes a time when you know things aren't going to get better, that there's no coming back. So, I did the kind thing.

I'll stand before God Himself and answer for what I've done.

I'll have some questions of my own. ✸

The work wasn't a challenge.
It was the people he had
no clue about.

Lab

Neil liked being in the lab at night. It was quiet, and no one expected anything from him.

It wasn't that he didn't belong; his test scores put him at the top of his class. The *work* wasn't a challenge. It was the *people* he had no clue about.

Mary's work in laser optimization was interesting, but the way she got along with everyone amazed him. She acted like she had never met a stranger, except when she met Neil. It wasn't for lack of trying on her part. Neil just didn't know how to respond.

Darin's work in narrow-field data transmission was groundbreaking, but he could also tell a story that could keep a group spellbound, leaning forward in their seats, so they could hear what came next that much sooner. That astonished Neil.

This wasn't a new situation for him. School had been a minefield of social awkwardness, but he had hoped that somehow, magically, his life after school would be different. The only difference was that he was no longer surrounded by people his own age, but by various generations, which was just another complicating factor. He had no clue on how to treat older people like peers.

As he compiled his latest attempts at the linguistic subroutine, he reflected on the irony of the least social of his group was working on making the project's interface more "human."

"Hello, Neil," the computer said as he launched the program.

At least I have you, he thought. ✪

Am I mourning? Should I be?

Void

I feel your absence now more than I ever felt your presence. That's on me. I'll take responsibility for that. Did that factor into your decision, I wonder?

If it did, I'm sorry. It's far too little way too late, but it's there, if that makes any difference. I've learned my lesson, but the chance to use that knowledge is gone. It's too late, I know.

Still, for every bit of sadness, there's one of anger. Anger at me, and anger at you.

It was selfish of you, is what I tell myself I'm feeling now. Selfish that you would voluntarily do this to me. This was a choice, not some whim of fate or bad luck or an angry god. You chose this for both of us. Did you think of me when you came to your decision? Did I even cross your mind?

I tell myself that I need to move on. Staring at a clock wishing it to go backwards is a waste of time. You made your decision, and I'm living in the aftermath. So, time to start living.

Am I mourning? Should I be? Was yours a mourn-able action? I'm caught in the middle of anger and sadness, in the lukewarm noth-ingness. I know I'll feel both, and I dread it as much as I yearn for it.

Every space you touched is now touched by your absence. The car, the house, the bed. All are different, now. Filled with the void you left. ☾

"Maybe if you said something worth listening to," she muttered under her breath — but not quite under enough.

Headphones

Abby's headphones were her lifeline.

Since humans couldn't shut their ears like they could their eyes — a design flaw, in her opinion — she liked to be able to control her surroundings the best she could, and the headphones accomplished the task. She saved her money and bought the best pair she could. They were *hers*.

She liked to listen to different kinds of music, melodies that let her know there was a world out there unlike the world she experienced every day. Upbeat, happy meaningless songs when she knew her parents were fighting. Beautiful, classical music when people were ugly to her at school. The teachers didn't like her wearing them in the hall, but no one had actually taken the headphones away from her.

That was, until one day, her mother came up the stairs, stormed into her room, and yanked them off her head.

"What?" Abby said, too suddenly cut off from her world and thrust into the other.

"I've been yelling at you to come downstairs for dinner for 10 minutes," she said. "Food's cold, and we're tired of you not listening to us."

"Maybe if you said something worth listening to," she muttered under her breath — but not quite under enough.

She had never seen that look of anger on her mother's face.

Her mother looked around the room, found a pair of scissors and cut the headphone's cord.

"Eat or don't," her mother said, tossing the ruined headphones to her. "Your choice."

And she left. ✪

"Less mess, and, I'll be honest, it just viscerally feels like it would hurt him more to be shredded than burned."

Shredded

So, how much shredding power are you looking for?"

Cynthia looked at the office store employee as if he were speaking a different language.

"Ma'am?"

"The normal amount of shredding, I suppose."

"Well, we have different levels of shredding for different needs," he said, undeterred. He went to one end of the shredder display. "This one, for example, is an eight sheet, cross-cut shredder, great for home needs or very light office work." He then stepped over to far side of the display. "Now this bad boy, on the other hand, is an 18 sheet, guaranteed jam-proof powerhouse." He pulled out the waste bin full of sample shreddings, looked at her and smiled. "Instant confetti, ready for New Years Eve," he said.

"When you say 'sheets,' how many photos would that be?" Cynthia asked.

"Photos? Well, they're thicker than paper, so figure about half, I guess. You have a lot....?"

"My husband left me for someone half our age two days ago," Cynthia said. "We were married for 25 years, so, yes, there are quite a few photos that I'd like gone, and I like the idea of shredding, more than, say, burning. Less mess, and, I'll be honest, it just viscerally feels like it would hurt him more to be shredded than burned."

He looked at her for a moment, as if deciding what to say next. "Well," he said, moving to the middle of the display, "I'd think that this 12-sheet model would work fine." ⟲

His ideas were like sandcastles;
impossible to move
without crumbling.

Small

The world was too big today.

It was the feeling of being a mote of dust in a world too large for such a thing to matter. He knew it was coming. It was familiar in a way that he wished it hadn't been, but he could feel its approach hours before. He knew the signs, he could sense its arrival and prepare the best he could. Still, *remembering* the feeling was a pale shade of the actual experience.

In better times, in happier moods, he felt that he could do almost anything with enough effort and enough passion. Nothing was out of reach if he wanted it badly enough. The world was small and lithe and would bend to his will.

Now, though, gravity had increased. What was supple turned brittle. His ideas were like sandcastles; impossible to move without crumbling.

It was times like this where he could step outside of himself, for a brief moment, and look at what he was. He knew what he was feeling wasn't real. Nothing had changed in the world except for his outlook. His internal works. For that moment, he felt the hope that this feeling would pass as soon as it had arrived.

But the moment would always end too soon. There were no short-cuts in outrunning the shadow. It would take effort that he currently couldn't summon.

The world refused to shrink down to a manageable size, so he did the only thing he knew to do.

He waited. ✪

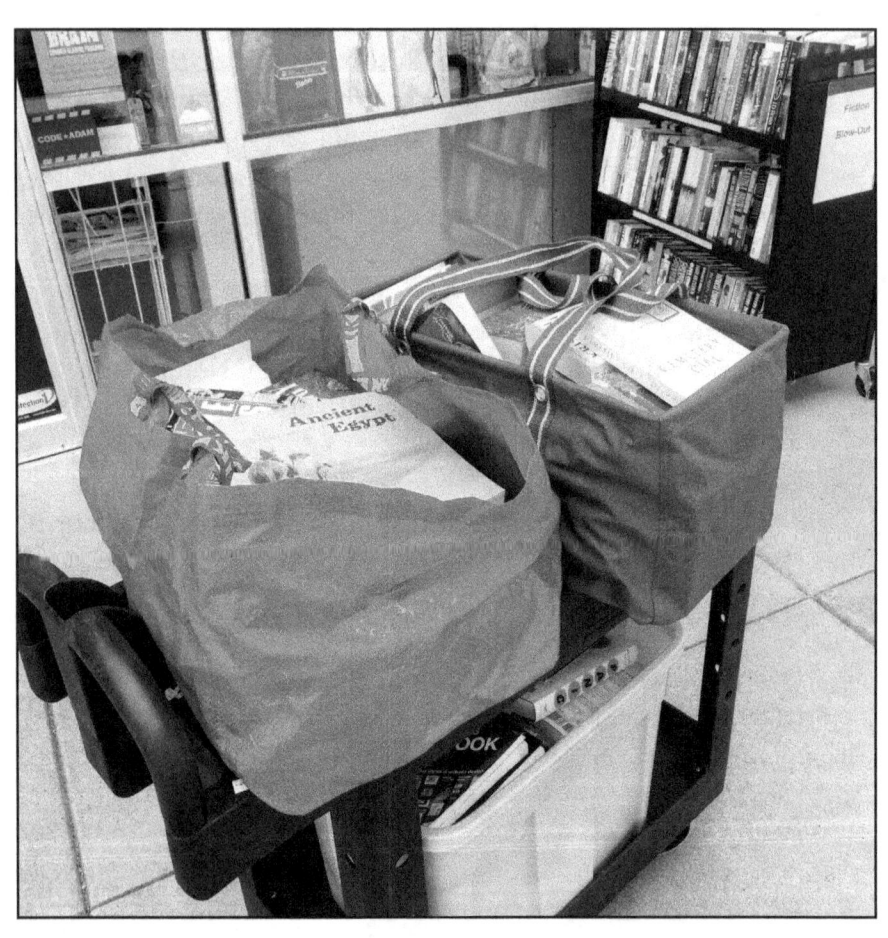

"Think of all the knowledge
that's on this cart," Matt said.
"Knowledge that we'll
never absorb."

Books

"It seems like a defeat," Matt said, putting the sack of books on the cart.

"What does?" Lynn asked, handing him the next sack out of the trunk.

"Just acknowledging that we're never going to read these," he said. He looked at the hundred or so books they were piling on the second-hand book reseller's cart. It hadn't seemed like so many while they were going through their purge at home, but here, on the sidewalk in the bright light of day, seeing them all together, it was an impressive pile. "It feels like we're giving up."

"You wanted to do some spring cleaning," she said. "And we both have a book problem. I'm tired of seeing how much we can cram into the bookshelves. It'd be nice to be able to use bookends for a change."

"Think of all the knowledge that's on this cart," Matt said. "Knowledge that we'll never absorb."

"If it was just a matter of absorbing it," Lynn said, handing him the last bag, "it wouldn't be a problem. Thing is, we're never going to read these."

"They seemed like good ideas when we bought them," he said.

"But we never *read* them," she said, slamming the trunk closed for emphasis. "Look, maybe it's a feeling of mortality. It's not that we don't want to read them. It's that we don't have *time* to read them. We can only read so many books in our life."

"So, prioritization."

"Yep. We're just picking our battles." ⚙

When the doctors start talking
about "comfort" instead of
"healing," that gets your attention.

Deathbed

They always say what you'll feel when you're on your deathbed, or what you want to avoid feeling. "Nobody on their deathbed ever wished they'd spent more time at work," and that sort of thing.

The truth is that nobody, except the extremely morbid, *truly* imagines they'll ever be on their own deathbed. Sure, family and friends may pass on — the older you get, the more that particular train builds speed — but you never, in your heart of hearts, think it'll be *you*.

Until, of course, it is.

And so, I find myself on my deathbed. Something changes when it goes from metaphorical to literal. I'm lying in the bed in which, assuming I don't fall out of it at some point, I will breathe my last.

I'm lucky I'm home. My deathbed is the bed I had slept in for years; I just never knew it. Is that ironic? I can't tell.

The doctors have all signed off, making sure that I and my family had everything I needed for the rest of my life. When the doctors start talking "comfort" instead of "healing," that gets your attention.

Friends — the brave ones, anyway — have stopped by to say good bye, even if they don't say those words. Family looks suitably stricken. I'd spare my family this if I could. Hell, I'd get *up* if I could.

And what am I thinking of as the clock winds down?

It's the feeling of walking out of a movie before it ends. ⟁

About the Author

David Falkirk is, among other things, an author, designer, photographer, editor, husband, son, responsible pet owner, recovering journalist, podcaster and a proud geek from strong Scottish stock.

He is the author of *Fast 40 — Vol. 2: Within, Without* and *Fast 40 — Vol. 3: The Shapes of Belief.* His first novel will be released in 2016.

For more information, or to join his newsletter for free stories, updates, and pointers to things he believes are cool (and may very well be), visit www.davidfalkirk.com.

INDEX
(Fast 40, Volumes 1-3)

For updates, free stories and other things of interest,
join up by clicking "newsletter" at www.davidfalkirk.com.
It comes complete with a "no spam" guarantee.

www.ingramcontent.com/pod-product-compliance
Lightning Source LLC
Chambersburg PA
CBHW070507130626
46555CB00003B/1193